THE NINE LIVES OF
FURRY PURRY
BEANCAT

THE
LIBRARY
CAT

PHILIP

More
Furry Purry Beancat
adventures!

THE PIRATE CAPTAIN'S CAT

THE RAILWAY CAT

THE WITCH'S CAT
— coming soon!

THE NINE LIVES OF FURRY PURRY BEANCAT

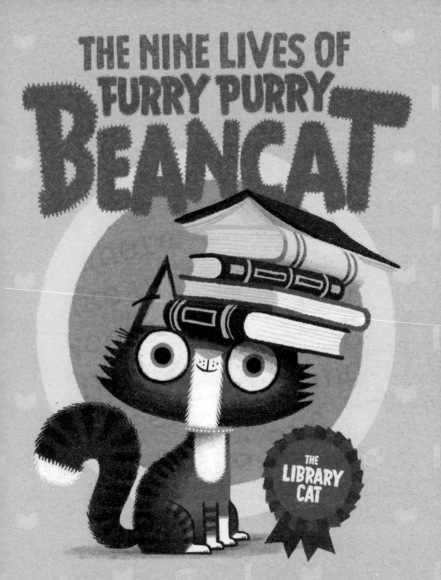

THE
LIBRARY
CAT

PHILIP ARDAGH

Illustrated by

Rob Biddulph

SIMON & SCHUSTER

First published in Great Britain in 2021 by Simon & Schuster UK Ltd

1 3 5 7 9 10 8 6 4 2

Simon & Schuster UK Ltd
1st Floor, 222 Gray's Inn Road
London
WC1X 8HB

www.simonandschuster.co.uk
www.simonandschuster.com.au
www.simonandschuster.co.in

Simon & Schuster Australia, Sydney
Simon & Schuster India, New Delhi

A CIP catalogue record for this book is available from the British Library.

PB ISBN 978-1-4711-8407-9
eBook ISBN 978-1-4711-8408-6

Printed and bound by CPI Group (UK) Ltd, Croydon, CR0 4YY

MIX
Paper from
responsible sources
FSC® C020471

For librarians everywhere
Philip Ardagh

For Deeley and Ballou
Rob Biddulph

Furry Purry Beancat found a patch of sunlight, followed her tail round in a circle three times, then settled herself down in a furry ball of purry cat. She yawned, lowered her head to the ground and pulled her beautiful fluffy tail in front of her little pink nose.

Where will I wake up next? she wondered, slowly closing her big green eyes and drifting off to sleep . . .

CHAPTER 1
ON THE SHELF!

Furry Purry Beancat opened her big green eyes and found herself face to face with a spider snoozing in his web. He had many eyes and all of them were closed. Beancat felt the tickle of dust in her little pink nose and tried not to sneeze. But she couldn't stop herself.

It was rather an impressive sneeze, causing some of the strands of the spider's web to break and the whole thing to wobble like a trampoline. The spider opened all his eyes at once and glared at Furry Purry Beancat. The effect was a bit like someone suddenly turning all the lights on.

'Yeah, thanks for that, Furry,' said the spider gloomily. 'Nothing like being woken by a sneeze. Gives me such a boost.' He sighed.

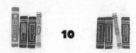

He's used my name. My first name, Furry Purry Beancat thought. *Which means that we must be friends on first-name terms. Only I don't know what his name is . . .*

Now, not knowing the name of one of your friends might seem odd, but the really important thing you need to know about Furry Purry Beancat is that when she falls asleep (which she does rather a lot) she sometimes – only sometimes, mind – wakes up somewhere completely different, in another one of her nine lives! And it ALWAYS ends up being an adventure, which is good because, apart from eating and sleeping, having adventures is what Furry Purry Beancat does best.

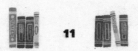

'Sorry I sneezed on you,' she said to the spider. 'It's the dust.'

'It's always the dust,' said the spider. 'You can't expect Reenie to reach all the way up here, can you?'

'Of course not,' replied Furry Purry Beancat, even though she didn't have a clue who Reenie was.

Furry Purry Beancat looked around to take in her surroundings. *Hmmm. She appeared to be on top of a bookcase, a very high bookcase, and it was one of many. There were bookcases everywhere. Some were against walls. Some were in the middle of the room with shelves on either side. Every shelf was full of books.*

Is this a bookshop? she wondered. *No,*

I think it's a public library! That means Reenie must be the library cleaner.

'Are you going to sneeze on me again?' asked the spider gloomily. 'It's just that it would be useful to know if you're planning to start the day with a fun-packed Let's-Sneeze-on-Gregory session.' He said the word 'fun-packed' as though it was more depressing than a bag full of custard cream biscuits where someone had licked off all the fillings.

'I did say sorry, Gregory,' said Furry Purry Beancat, as though she'd known his name all along.

'No time for apologies!' said Gregory. 'There are repairs to be made. It never stops!' He scuttled over to one of the

broken threads and set to work.

'See you later!' said Beancat.

'I expect so,' said the spider, 'unless I get vacuumed up or slammed shut in a book.'

Beancat smiled to herself. She suspected that Gregory the spider was one of those creatures who rather ENJOYED being gloomy!

'Then be careful,' she said.

'What excellent advice. Thank you, Furry. If you hadn't suggested that I might have gone swimming in a boiling kettle or—'

Beancat didn't wait to hear the rest. She made a graceful leap to the floor, her four white paws landing silently on a rug shaped like an enormous lemon. At that moment

a woman appeared through an open door marked STAFF ONLY.

'Good mornin', Furry!' she said with a beautiful voice that sounded to Beancat like music. 'Sleep well?'

'*Meow!*' said Beancat, and rubbed round the woman's legs. She was wearing fabulously shiny black shoes.

The woman bent down and gave Furry Purry Beancat a splendid stroke

from head to tail a few times and then a VERY professional rub under the chin.

'Ready for breakfast?' she asked, turning and walking back through the doorway.

'*Meow!*' said Beancat, trotting alongside the woman.

They went past a door marked CARETAKER and into a room with a table and chairs, a kitchen sink, a microwave oven and a few kitchen cabinets. There was a door to the outside, next to which was a row of large old-fashioned coat pegs.

This must be where the library staff go to relax, thought Beancat. *A staffroom.*

The only strange thing about the room – and it WAS very strange indeed – was a large beanstalk, with great big leaves the

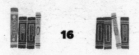

size of dinner plates growing up the wall. Obviously, it wasn't a *real* beanstalk but that wasn't the point.

What's THAT doing here? Beancat wondered.

The woman opened one of the cupboards and brought out a pouch of cat food and two cat bowls. One had a paw-print pattern circling the other side and, much to her delight, the other one had FURRY PURRY BEANCAT painted on it.

One of the Rs was a little squished, and she guessed that whoever had painted it must originally have written: FURY PURRY BEANCAT.

Then they'd realized that they'd left out one of the Rs and had to make a quick correction!

But Furry Purry Beancat didn't mind; she was VERY PLEASED that someone had gone to the trouble at all.

In one swift moment the woman had the bowl on the floor, the food in the bowl and the empty sachet and its torn-off top in the pedal bin. Now she had the fridge door open and, before you could say, 'Thirsty?', Beancat found the other bowl filled with full-fat milk.

The door of the fridge was covered in fridge magnets. Lots of them were of cats. There was also one with a curved palm tree on a patch of very yellow sand on which was

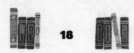

written TRINIDAD & TOBAGO and one of a teddy bear reading a book with I LOVE BOOKS on its cover. A few of them held pieces of paper to fridge door. Beancat caught a glimpse of some of the bigger words:

Save the county's libraries!

There was also a takeaway menu for somewhere called THE CHICKEN SHACK.

But Beancat was FAR more interested in her *own* food. She purred as she ate.

The outside door opened and in walked a much younger woman.

'Morning, Marcia!' she said to the first lady.

'Mornin', Lizzie,' replied the lady Furry Purry Beancat now knew to be Marcia.

The two women looked to Beancat as if they couldn't be more different. Marcia had a fantastic frizz of thick black hair with a zigzag-patterned scarf tied round it, while Lizzie's hair was very neat and very ginger and cut very straight at the bottom. Marcia wore a fabulous dress of brilliant colours and Lizzy had simple dark blue jeans and a blue T-shirt.

Beancat thought Marcia looked like one of those people who was saying to the world, *Hello! I'm here and I'm happy! Standing out and outstanding!* Lizzie, by contrast, looked like someone who was happy to blend in.

Lizzie scratched Beancat on the head. 'Morning, Furry!' she said.

Furry Purry Beancat didn't stop eating – she'd no idea she'd been hungry until she'd smelled the food – but she did some EVEN LOUDER PURRING to show Lizzie some appreciation.

The next person through the door was very different to the first two.

He was a *he* for a start. He was tallish and thinnish and looked youngish. Beancat wasn't very good at guessing humans' ages, but she thought this person was more of a boy than a man, even though he towered above everyone and everything in the library staffroom apart from the cupboard on the wall to the right of the sink.

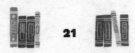

That makes him tall *not* tallish, thought Beancat, adjusting her first impressions.

He wore brown corduroy trousers – the material that looks like a ploughed field – and a white shirt with a button-down collar and a green tie, which, like him, was long and thin.

'Hi, Dave!' said Marcia and Lizzie.

'Morning,' said Dave.

Furry Purry Beancat stopped eating and looked directly at Dave. Not because he sounded almost as gloomy as Gregory the spider but because, in that one word – the way he'd said it – she *knew* that Dave didn't like cats.

Cats just know, you know. They can tell whether you're:

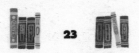

- a cat lover
- someone who enjoys fussing over a cat when they see one
- someone who doesn't really like or dislike them
- someone who does NOT like cats

And it was obvious to Furry Purry Beancat that Dave was in this final cat-e-gory!

So, what did she do?

What *any* cat would do.

She went straight over to him and rubbed the bottom of his brown trousers.

'Good morning, cat,' he said.

Please don't think that Furry Purry Beancat was giving Dave special attention

because she wanted him to like her. No. Beancat is not a dog.

Dogs spend most of their lives trying to please their humans and thinking, *Love me, love me, love me, love meeeeeeee!* They dream about their humans and, when they wake up, the first thing they think about is MAKING SURE THEIR HUMANS LOVE THEM.

I hate to tell you this . . . but Beancat thinks that dogs aren't the shiniest tins on the pet-food shelf.

 25

Cats know that it's a real PRIVILEGE for you to be in the company of a cat and may give you the HONOUR of their sitting in your lap once in a while! But cats are drawn to people who don't like them like rabbits to a supermarket with a special offer on carrots. They want to get cat hair all over their clothes for starters . . .

Soon Marcia, Lizzie and Dave were sitting round the staffroom table, each with a hot drink. Beancat's little pink nose was filled with the smells of tea and coffee. It soon became obvious to her – because there's no denying that she's a very clever cat – that Marcia was the librarian in charge, Lizzie was a librarian too and that Dave the Cat-Hater was some kind of library assistant.

They were talking about the weekend. Lizzie and Dave had both been on a SAVE THE COUNTY'S LIBRARIES march in town. From what Beancat could gather there had been balloons and bands and speeches and lots of people carrying banners arguing for the importance of local libraries.

'Do you think there may be plans to close this library?' Liz asked Marcia.

'I've heard whispers,' said Marcia, 'but, then again, most librarians are worried that it's THEIR library that might be closed down . . . But enough of this. Time to plan the day ahead!' said Marcia. 'We've got three classes in this mornin', haven't we?'

Lizzie nodded. 'That's right.'

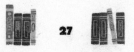

'Don't forget to tell 'em about the Summer Fun activities for the holidays, righ'? And give their teachers them leaflets.'

'Right,' said Lizzie. 'Will do.'

The more Furry Purry Beancat heard Marcia speak, the more she LOVED Marcia's voice. It made her want to sing!

Beancat fancies herself as a bit of a singer. All cats do.

Now, Beany thinks she's beautiful.

And she is.

Beany also thinks she deserves all the loving and the stroking she gets.

And she does.

But when it comes to her singing, Beany is plain WRONG.

In her head she sounds like a professional

opera singer mimicking the song of the skylark.

But to anyone in earshot what she actually sounds like is someone having a fight with a set of bagpipes, or a howler monkey with a slow puncture.

If you've ever heard a cat wailing at night, then you'll know what Furry Purry Beancat's singing sounds like . . .

. . . and cat-wailing is NOT a good sound.

It doesn't encourage people to leap to their feet, throw flowers and shout, 'Encore!' (which is a posh way of saying, 'More!').

No. It encourages people to leap to their feet, throw open a window and then throw an old boot in the direction of the noise.

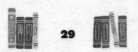

But, blissfully unaware of this sad truth, Beancat was beginning to daydream about her and Marcia singing duets together.

Being a library cat is going to be a nice, peaceful life, thought Beany. *A chance to relax and unwind.*

Furry Purry Beancat was about as wrong as it was possible to be.

CHAPTER 2
OPENING TIME

The clock showed fifteen minutes to nine o'clock. The three human staff round the table got to their feet and left the room. The fourth member of staff – a particularly furry, *purry* member of staff – trotted out after them, glancing at the huge beanstalk as she went.

She watched Marcia and Lizzie go behind a counter and do whatever it was that they needed to do before opening for the day.

Eventually, Marcia called out, 'Doors, please, Dave!'

Dave, who had been pushing around a wooden trolley of books that he was putting on the shelves one at a time, walked briskly through the foyer, then unlocked and opened the two huge front doors.

Beancat followed him across the black-and-white-tiled floor and stuck her nose outside. There was a small car park and then some fields. She breathed in the morning air, her super-sensitive cat nose sucking up useful information about the

area. Beancat uses her nose a bit like the internet, accessing information and storing it away.

Here, for example are just ten of the things she could smell the second the doors were opened:

- 🐾 Fields – grass, mud, bark, flowers, trees
- 🐾 People – different scents, materials, shampoo
- 🐾 Cowpats – some fresher than others
- 🐾 Car exhausts – nasty, strong and unhealthy
- 🐾 Dog wee – typical dogs, marking what they wished was their territory
- 🐾 Birds – different types and sizes, the strongest smell being of pigeon

🐾 Wet paint – colour unknown!

🐾 Car park – tarmac, oil leaks, petrol, plastic upholstery

🐾 Bins – very SMELLY indeed

What do you mean that's only nine smells?

One, two, three, four . . . Okay, you're right. But some of the smells were made up of lots of *other* smells!

Three people were waiting just outside for the doors of the library to open.

The first was an elderly gentleman, wearing an old suit with a frayed blue shirt and carrying a worn leather briefcase tucked under one arm. He smelled of shaving foam, though his razor had missed a few patches of bristle

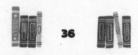

on his chin and there were a few nicks where he'd cut himself.

'Good morning, Furry Purry Beancat!' he said. 'Another beautiful day!' He had a thick accent that made his English a little harder to understand. It came out as: *Good mornink, Vurry Purry Bincat. Anuzzer beautiful day!*

Beancat purrrrrred.

'Good morning, Mr Pasternak,' said Dave.

'Good morning, Dave,' said the elderly gentleman. 'Good to see you at the Save Libraries march on Saturday.'

'You too, Mr Pasternak,' said Dave.

Next, there was a lady with snow-white hair who was pulling a tartan wheelie-

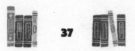

trolley behind her. She wore glasses with such thick lenses that they made her eyes look big and googly!

'Hello puss-puss,' she said to Beancat in a voice that people often seem to use when talking to cats. 'Morning, Dave!'

'Good morning, Joan,' said Dave.

Beancat was rather pleased that Joan had greeted her *before* she had greeted Dave. This was a woman who got her priorities right!

The third person looked to Beancat to be about the same age as Dave. He smiled down at Beancat. It was the look of someone looking at Beancat for the first time. He was wearing grey trousers, a white shirt and an autumn-brown sweater.
He seemed a little nervous.

He said nothing to Dave but walked up to the counter.

'Good mornin',' said Marcia. 'How can I help you?'

'Good morning, madam,' said the young man. 'Do I need a library card to read in the library?'

'Not at all,' said Marcia. 'Everyone's welcome to use the library. You only need a card if you wantta take some books away with you.'

'So I may just sit and read?'

''Course! That's what libraries are here for. An' if you needs help with anything, please ask me or one of the staff. You'll recognize us from these.' She held up the badge hanging round her neck.

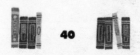

'Thank you, most kindly,' said the young man. He went to look round.

I think I'd better explore too, thought Furry Purry Beancat, *as I'm SUPPOSED to know my way around here already.*

In the historical romance section, she saw a spider dropping on a thread from above.

'Hello, Gregory!' she said.

'WHAT DID YOU JUST CALL ME?' asked a very INDIGNANT spider. Her eyes – all of them – narrowing in annoyance. 'It's me. Daphne!'

'Oh,' said Beancat. 'Sorry, Daphne . . . From a distance I thought you were Gregory.'

'I don't look anything like the old gloombag,' snapped Daphne. 'I'm FAR more beautiful.'

'Yes, well, sorry about that,' said Furry Purry Beancat.

'You haven't FORGOTTEN about our secret meeting, have you?' asked Daphne. Her many eyes narrowed again.

'No. Of course not. No,' said Beancat. *What secret meeting?* she wondered. *What do me and a spider have to discuss?*

'Good,' said Daphne. 'See you in the caretaker's office in about half an hour.'

I don't know about cats in general, but luckily Beancat is very good at telling the time without needing a clock. (And not just mealtimes, which, if she had her way,

would be most of the time.)

So, for the next half hour, Beancat went on patrol.

She found the tables with the daily newspapers on them, with a few comfy chairs dotted around them where people could sit and read.

She found a room with a row of computers on desks against a wall.

She discovered a small reference section, an area with lots of leaflets, and an area with books about local history, and huge bound copies of local newspapers. (They were copies of the *Gothport Chronicle* going back almost two hundred years.) On the wall was a large framed brown-and-white photograph showing people dressed

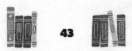

FURRY, THE

in old-fashioned clothes standing on a brown-and-white-tiled floor, and next to that hung an old map of the county.

Then she discovered a children's section through an open archway. It was bright and colourful and instantly inviting. There were huge multicoloured cushions on the floor in one corner, some wooden boxes shaped like a train and train carriages filled

LIBRARY CAT

with picture books and – all along one wall, above the rows of shelves – were pictures and drawings done by children. And each and every one was of her!

Every picture, whether drawn with felt-tip pens, wax crayons, poster paints or watercolours, was of Furry Purry Beancat! Written in cut-out letters above them was FURRY, THE LIBRARY CAT.

She was a superstar!

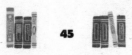

Furry Purry Beancat gave SUCH a loud PURR that Marcia came out from behind the counter and stuck her head through the archway to see what was happening.

'Oh, it's YOU, Furry!' she laughed. 'I thought something was wrong with the boiler you's purring so LOUD!'

Furry Purry Beancat trotted over, tail held high and rubbed herself round Marcia's legs.

'If I didn't know better, I'd think you've been admirin' them pictures of yourself again!'

That's precisely what I have been doing, thought Beancat.

Marcia looked at her watch. 'Some of

your fans should be here any minute! I don't know what they'll do if this library does close down.'

Furry Purry Beancat stopped purring and looked up at her. *Is there something you're not telling the others?* she wondered. *Are you worried that this may be one of the libraries they close down?*

Beancat's thoughts were interrupted a few minutes later when a class of small children came swarming in. They headed straight for the children's library and straight for Furry Purry Beancat.

They had obviously been given VERY good instructions for how to treat her and followed them well. No one pushed and shoved or tried to pull her tail. After they

had given her plenty of loving attention, their teacher called them together.

'Okay, Orange Class. Everyone choose one book and take it up to the counter. Don't forget to tell the librarians your last name, so they can find your library card and stamp your book for you. And what will the stamp tell you?'

'When to bring it back by!' the children chorused.

'Good,' said the teacher. 'Now, get choosing.'

Soon, all of Orange Class were eagerly scanning the shelves for books. All except one boy who was looking at Furry Purry Beancat. He couldn't take his eyes off her.

Beancat strolled over, her beautifully

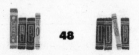

fluffy tail held high.

He put out a small hand and touched her. *Hello, Beancat*, he said.

Hello, Timmy, she said. Then . . . *Wow!*

It took Beancat a moment to realize that the boy hadn't spoken out loud. How could she have heard him speak inside her head? And how had she known his name was Timmy? Beancat needed to process the information to make sense of what had just happened.

There is a very rare group of people who can talk to cats. And by that I mean have an actual proper conversation: hearing and understanding the cat's response. This may come as a surprise to you, unless you're one of them yourself or know someone who is.

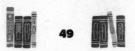

Some children have the gift but, for whatever reason, when they grow older, they lose it. They will always love cats and have a special relationship with them but can no longer speak to them directly.

And this direct communication is a strange experience for the cat too.

You look very beautiful today, Furry Purry Beancat, Timmy's voice said inside Beancat's head.

Thank you, replied Beancat. She purred.

Timmy laughed. *I can feel that through your fur!*

A woman came over and stood in front of Timmy. 'Time to choose your book now, Timmy,' she said with a smile, her hands dancing in front of her as she spoke.

And off he went!

Beancat thought about the woman with the dancing hands. Why had she done that? Timmy had certainly been watching

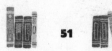

them – her fingers forming different shapes – as she spoke.

Beancat jumped up on to a table with a display of books about dinosaurs. She weaved between the upright books without so much as touching one. An excellent catty skill. She could do it without thinking but it always seemed to impress people!

She watched the class excitedly looking through the books, some showing each other what they had chosen, others showing the teacher. She watched Timmy and the woman with the dancing hands.

He can't hear, Beancat realized. *Timmy can't hear. The woman is speaking to him*

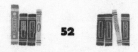

CHAPTER 3
'MAKING PLANS!'

eenie was a wiry woman: small, thin but tough, and she was a demon with a duster! She sprayed, she polished, she dusted, she wiped. Her hair was completely white but for a single streak of blue like a go-faster stripe on a racing car. She wore a nylon housecoat of a lighter blue than the streak in her hair. On it was proudly pinned an enamel brooch of a thistle: the emblem of Scotland.

Reenie wiped shelves, book spines, windowsills, countertops . . . Her job seemed never-ending. She had a little carpet sweeper – like a vacuum cleaner without the electrics – which she'd push around to sweep up the odd muddy footprint. Her eyes scoured the carpet like a bird of prey looking down on the landscape for its next meal . . . but her victims were sweet papers or anything else that shouldn't be there.

Now and again she'd stop and chat to someone she obviously knew who had come to use the library. She had a soft Scottish accent that, to Beancat's ears, sounded beautiful. Some of the people she chatted with were the same sort of age as Reenie – Beancat thought of that as 'granny age' – and some of them were teenagers. Everyone spoke quietly and, nine times out of ten, the conversation would take place with Reenie clutching a cloth or a yellow feather duster.

She greeted Mr Pasternak by name with a polite nod, but let him be. He had made himself very comfortable in a corner with a desk and chair. He had a pile of library books next to him and was writing things

down with an old-fashioned fountain pen on to a pad of lined paper.

He seems a busy, thought Beancat. Reenie must know not to disturb him.

Reenie also said 'Good morning!' to the polite young man who'd asked Marcia if he could use the library even though he didn't have a card. He had a newspaper open and Beancat noticed that he was reading a section headed APPOINTMENTS.

'Good morning, madam,' he responded politely.

Reenie grinned. It was obvious that she didn't get called 'madam' very often, and she clearly LIKED it!

Furry Purry Beancat decided to get to know this newcomer a little better. With

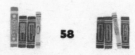

grace and elegance she jumped up on to the small low table on which a number of papers were displayed. The young man's face was behind the newspaper and he was obviously engrossed in what he was reading.

She reached out her front right paw and tapped her side of the newspaper. All four of her paws were white, which made it look as though she was wearing socks (all knee-length except for the one on her front left paw, which appeared to have slipped down to her ankle).

The man didn't respond.

Beancat tapped it again.

It made rather a satisfying noise.

So she bopped it again.

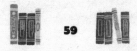

Bop! Bop! Bop! Bop! – pause –
Bop!

This got the desired result, but Beany's cat instincts took over – most cats DO like bopping things – and she carried on bopping a little longer than was strictly necessary.

Bop! **Bop!** **Bop!** **Bop! Bop!**

The young man lowered his paper. 'I saw you when I first arrived, Mistress Cat,' he said. 'That was most welcoming. Everyone – every*thing* – is most welcoming here. I feel most welcome. Is this your home?' He began stroking her. Beancat purred. 'You are most beautiful. Back home, I have a beautiful cat. Her name is Iishraq. It means "Sunshine". Sadly, I could not bring her with me.' He paused mid-stroke, halfway along Furry Purry Beancat's back.

He's thinking of his cat, she thought. *Good job he didn't bring her to the library with him. There's a no-pets rule . . . Hang on! How do I know that?* Then she caught a glimpse of the man's dark brown eyes. And she understood.

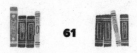

'Home' didn't mean the house or flat or room or wherever it was the man was living now. 'Home' didn't even mean this country. 'Home' meant *his* country; whatever country it was that he'd come from. A place he'd had to leave without bringing his beloved cat Iishraq with him. He'd had to leave his Sunshine behind.

'I see you made friends with Furry,' said Marcia, who was passing with a pile of books. 'She's our most popular member of staff, which we don't mind because she's our most popular co-worker too. As for me, I'm Marcia, the librarian.'

The man stood up and gave a slight bow of the head. 'My name is Yusuf, Marcia. You have a most pleasing library and I would

very much like to come here often.'

Marcia beamed. 'An' you'll be very welcome, Yusuf.'

Furry Purry Beancat heard a loud tutting sound and turned her head to see that Reenie had come upon a cobweb.

Spiders' web . . . Daphne! thought Beancat. She'd been so busy watching Reenie at work and getting to know Yusuf that she'd forgotten about her secret meeting!

She dashed through the doorway marked PRIVATE and **SQUEEEEZED** through the gap between the door frame and door into the caretaker's office.

It turned out it wasn't so much an office as the final resting place for broken furniture

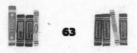

and a variety of other odds and ends.

'Oh, THERE you are,' said a gloomy voice. 'How kind of you to find time in your busy schedule to honour us with your presence, Furry.'

'Hello, Gregory,' said Beancat. The spider was sitting on a strut between the front legs of an up-turned chair. 'Sorry I'm late.'

'Better late than never, I suppose,' said Daphne, lowering herself from the ceiling. 'You can be so forgetful sometimes, Furry. I suppose we should be honoured you turned up at all.'

You try living nine lives, thought Furry Purry Beancat. *Not only not knowing which life you'll wake up in, but having no*

memory of it from before. 'Shall we get started?' she said.

'Says the one who was late and holding up proceedings,' grumped Gregory.

'Ignore him, Furry,' Daphne insisted. 'We need to plan.'

'Is this about the library being closed down?' asked Furry Purry Beancat.

'WHAT?' said Daphne and Gregory as one.

'They're closing the library?' said Gregory with a sigh. 'The first I've heard of it but, then again, I'm always the last to know. It's like the time when—'

'No . . . I mean, maybe . . . I mean, I don't know!' said Furry Purry Beancat. 'I thought that's what YOU were going to TELL me.'

Daphne fixed Beancat in a stare, which, what with her being a spider and all, involved a LOT of unblinking eyes. 'Don't tell me you've forgotten, Beancat?' she said. 'Tomorrow is the first Thursday of the month, and the first Thursday of the month is the day Reenie gets her supplies.'

Furry Purry Beancat had NO idea what Daphne was on about, of course. She had to think fast. *Reenie is the cleaner*, she thought, *so it's likely that these are cleaning supplies we're talking about . . .*

'If we can't think of a way of getting rid of that spray before she has a chance to use

it, me and Gregory will be dead before you can say "squirt a spider",' said Daphne.

'You make it sound such FUN,' said Gregory sadly.

Bug killer? thought Beancat. *Reenie has ordered a can of bug spray!*

This was serious. It could be a matter of life and death!

'Remind me why you don't just move out?' asked Beancat.

'We've been through this, Furry,' said Daphne, blinking each and every one of her eyes at exactly the same

time. 'This is our home. We're LIBRARY spiders. Our families have lived here since the library opened. My ancestors grew up hearing the **CHER-CHUNK** of the date stamp, the **SH-SH-SHUFFLING** of the brown cards, later replaced with the **BLEEP** of the card reader. This is OUR land! No one has the right to make us move!'

'No, quite,' said Beancat. 'Of course they don't. But my worry is that even if we can make the bug spray disappear, Reenie will simply order some more for the next delivery.'

'True. But that will give us until the first Thursday of NEXT month to worry about what to do next. The most important thing is to make sure that she doesn't get this

FIRST can,' said Daphne.

'I saw Reenie take out her cleaning things from the bottom cupboard in the staffroom earlier,' said Beancat. 'It's a sliding door so I might – *might* – be able to push it open, find the spray and knock it on to the floor . . . but I'm not sure what we do after that!'

'The sound will probably attract attention and the plan will be doomed to failure,' said – you guessed it – Gregory. 'We'll be dead before nightfall.'

'Oh, dooooooo be quiet, Gregory!' said Daphne. 'If you don't have anything useful to add—'

'I know,' said Gregory. 'Keep quiet. You want me to keep quiet.'

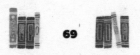

'Yes,' said Daphne.

'Say nothing.'

'Yes.'

'Keep schtum.'

'Schtum?'

'Schtum . . . Zip my lip.'

'Yes.'

'Shut my cakehole.'

'Er, Gregory,' said Furry Purry Beancat.

'Yes, Furry?'

'The plan. Can we get back to the plan?'

'Fine,' said Gregory gloomily. 'Please continue.'

'Right,' said Daphne. 'The—'

'I won't say another word.'

'Thank you—'

'I know when I'm not wanted.'

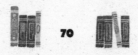

'It's not—'

'I'm here as a spectator not a participant,' said Gregory.

'THE PROBLEM,' said Furry Purry Beancat LOUDLY, 'will be if the sliding door is slid right across. If it's shut. It's not designed for cats to open. If there's a gap, I can wiggle my paw in there –' she demonstrated in mid-air – 'and then get my body weight behind it. And, even if I can get the door open and the can out of the cupboard, I still have to find a way to get rid of it.'

'So how do we make sure that it's kept open?' said Gregory.

'I have an idea,' said Beancat, 'but it may require a distraction that makes Reenie forget to shut it.'

'A distraction?' asked Daphne. 'Will that involve us?'

'It might do,' said Furry Purry Beancat, 'so it won't be without danger.'

'Oh, goodie,' said Gregory with all the enthusiasm of a snowman on a sunbed. 'I love danger.'

He didn't sound like he meant it.

CHAPTER 4
GOOD NEWS AND BAD

Ten minutes before closing time, Marcia suddenly called out, 'The library closes in ten minutes!' and Beancat nearly jumped out of her furry, purry skin. She had been dreaming about lying in a warm sunny spot and woke up to find that it was true! She had been dozing in the historical

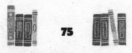

romance section on the floor next to a comfy chair Joan was sitting in with a pile of books next to her. 'Ten minutes!' Marcia repeated.

Furry Purry Beancat found herself joining in with a wail. She couldn't help it. She wanted the library users to enjoy the benefit of her beautiful voice too.

Joan's face broke into a wrinkly smile. 'As regular as clockwork!' she said.

I must always sing along when Marcia calls out that the library is closing, she thought. *What lucky people to hear me every day.*

Joan gave Beancat a scratch under the chin, which made them both very happy and Furry Purry Beancat even purrier.

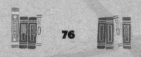

Beancat noticed that Joan had one of the books open on her lap and that there was a circle around the page number (which was thirty-five).

Beancat sniffed the page. It smelled of paper, tea – with milk – and, what was that? Bacon. Yes, bacon. Someone had once read the book while having breakfast!

What's the circled page number all about? Beancat wondered.

'Are you looking at my secret code, Furry?' asked Joan with a cackle, her great big googly eyes peering at her through her glasses. She lowered her voice. 'I used to keep a list of all the books I've read from here, but it got far too long. Now I always check page 35 and if, like this one, I've circled it, I know that I've read it before . . . Only in pencil, mind!'

It's amazing how many people tell cats their secrets. Perhaps it's because cats

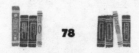

are obviously such intelligent, curious creatures. Or maybe it's because cats can't talk Human, so they won't tell anyone. Besides, even if they could talk Human, there are certain secrets – really important secrets – that cats would never tell anyone else. And, deep down, most people know that.

There was a giggle as a gaggle of schoolchildren left the computer corner where they'd been doing their homework. Beancat's ears swivelled into action.

"Night, Marcia!' one of the girls called out.

"Night, Patricia!' Marcia called back.

The last to leave was Mr Pasternak, his worn leather briefcase tucked under his

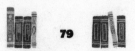

arm. 'Goodnight, ladies!' he said, before putting his hat on. 'See you tomorrow.'

Yusuf had left a few minutes before him, politely wishing everyone – including Beancat – a very nice evening.

It would be terrible if this library were closed, thought Beancat. *All these different people of different ages who get so much from it.* For the briefest moment her trademark purr turned to a growl.

A few minutes later, Dave was closing the doors to the library and sliding the bolts across.

Soon after that, Furry Purry Beancat was given her final meal of the day and Marcia switched the light off before leaving through the back door.

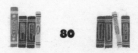

Now she had the library to herself. Well, mainly to herself. There were Gregory and Daphne, of course, and – she rather suspected – a whole host of other spiders she had yet to meet.

There was an under-fives' corner in the children's library with some rather nice big cushions in it, where children could sit and look at picture books. Furry had been eyeing them earlier and thought that they'd make rather a nice bed.

I'll have a proper explore later, she thought, *but, in the meantime, I'll have a quick nap.*

She gave a really good STRETCH, then settled down.

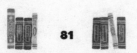

She awoke later to sound of shouting. High-pitched squeaky shouting.

'Oi, fatty! Clear off, you ball of fluff!'

I must still be dreaming, she thought, trying to settle back to sleep.

'Oi, YOU. Furry Purry Whatever Your Name Is! Clear off!'

Furry Purry Beancat opened a big green eye.

'Yes, YOU. I'm talking to you. We agreed. Now clear off!'

Beancat opened the other eye and scanned the darkness. *There!* There was the offender. Sitting on his haunches, in front of a row of books about pets, was a mouse. Brown and beady-eyed.

'You said you'd stay out of the children's library if I stayed out of sight all day and only came out after closing! You lied to me, you bag of fur!'

Well, he's brave, thought Beancat. *I'll give him that. One swipe from my paw and he's a goner.*

'And I suppose calling me names was part of the deal too?' she said.

'I'm only calling you names because you've broken your promise, you great big, whiskered whoppy-teller!'

Beancat gave a warning growl. 'Be nice!' she said.

'But,' said the mouse, sounding a little less sure of himself now, 'you did say that you'd leave us be.'

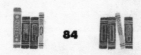

'If you say so,' said Beancat. She had no reason to believe that he was lying. She began ambling towards the entrance to the main library. 'But stick to your side of the deal.' If she saw the mouse running around the library in daylight, she might be expected to catch him! Beancat loved chasing things as much as the next cat, but she did NOT like the idea of being the resident mouse-catcher!

The library had a very different feel without people. The carpet somehow smelled stronger and more carpetty, and the bookstacks seemed to loom larger.

Daphne dropped out of nowhere and landed on the floor in front of her.

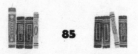

'How DO you do that?' asked a startled Furry Purry Beancat.

'Just one of my many skills,' said Daphne, wiping her face with a front leg. 'Did I hear Graham having one of his shouting matches?'

Graham must be the mouse, Beancat reasoned. 'I think I broke my side of our agreement,' she explained. 'Apparently, I agreed to stay out of the children's library after closing.'

'Apparently?' Daphne snorted. 'I remember the peace talks! Crumbs everywhere. I must live in the only library where a cat and a mouse make a treaty!'

'I'm all for peace, love and understanding . . . and food and sleep,' said Beancat.

'And adventure,' said Daphne. 'You told me that you like adventures!'

'I'll be having one of those tomorrow, trying to save you from the bug spray!' said Beancat.

Furry Purry Beancat's first big surprise the next morning was when a stranger came through the back door. Of course, everyone seemed a stranger to her when she first woke up in her library life, but she thought she'd met all the library staff: Marcia, Lizzie and Dave. And now here was a man in a blue suit, with thick black-rimmed spectacles and slicked-back white hair.

'Good morning, Furry!' he said with such

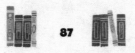

enthusiasm, bending down to greet her, that she found herself trotting over and nuzzling against him.

'Did you miss your old Reg?' he asked. 'I missed you!'

As Furry Purry Beancat rubbed her furry body against his bent legs, purring as loud as loud can be, she realized at once that this was HER human. Yes, Marcia and Lizzie were very

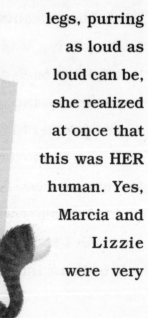

fond of her – loved her even – and she also 'belonged' to the library, but she knew – just KNEW – that she was Reg's cat, the library caretaker's cat.

'A present for you, my gorgeous girl!' he said, getting her special cat bowl from the cupboard, producing a small pot of cream and pouring some of it into the bowl.

Thank you, Reg! said Beancat, *'Meow!'*, and lapped it up.

'It's so good to be back, Furry. I was very well looked after in hospital. I saw one of the nurses who looked after our Jean –' he paused with a faraway look in his eye – 'but I couldn't wait to get back to the library and to you.'

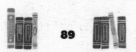

Now that Furry Purry had a beautifully oily tongue from all that cream, she began washing her paws.

Reg had bought a local paper from the newsagent on the corner and brought it in tucked under his arm. He placed it on the staffroom table and, after making himself a nice strong mug of tea, he sat down.

The headline read:

Local marathon cheat 'secretly wore rollerskates'

Underneath there was a photograph of a very puffed-out-looking man with a number thirteen pinned to his running shirt.

'A quick look at the news before I get

back into the swing of things,' said Reg. Though seated at the table, he left his chair at an angle, leaving his lap available for any furry, purry cats nearby.

Beancat jumped up on to it and settled down. Reg stroked her with one hand while holding his cup and turning the pages of the paper with the other.

'WHAT?' said Reg so loudly that Beancat stopped purring mid-purr.

What's wrong? she wondered.

'This can't be happening,' said Reg.

What is it? asked Beancat. *'Meow?'*

Reg jabbed the newspaper. 'Here,' he said. 'It says here that they're going to close the library.' He began reading the report out loud: *'In an exclusive interview with*

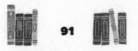

Gothport Chronicle *reporter, Dan Williams,* *Mayor Angela Haycroft has announced* *that Gothport Library is to close.* "We have *exciting plans for Gothport," she revealed,* *"and a new centre will be built housing* *a swimming pool, health spa and self-* *service library corner, launching Gothport* *Leisure into the twenty-first century."* Self-service library corner?!' said Reg, his face turning a very funny shade of purple. 'Is she MAD? This library is about so much more than books!'

Oh no! thought Beancat. *It's happened!* *Our worries have come true! Of course* *libraries are about so much more than* *books. They're a place for people like Mr* *Pasternak and Joan and Yusuf to come*

. . . and for the classes of schoolchildren, and those doing their homework . . . and for people to use computers. Who is this Mayor Angela Haycroft?

When Marcia and Lizzie and Dave arrived, there were mixed emotions. There were hugs and handshakes and happiness at Reg's unexpected return. From what was said Furry Purry Beancat realized that they weren't expecting him back until the following week.

'We were plannin' balloons and cake!' said Marcia.

'Which is why I came back early.' Reg smiled. 'I didn't want a fuss.'

Then there was the upset about the news of the plan to CLOSE THE LIBRARY.

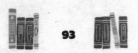

'This is crazy!' said Dave. 'On Saturday we were marching to save the county's libraries, and today we discover that ours is one they plan to close!'

'And the community will lose a PROPER library,' said Marcia. 'We ain't gonna take this lyin' down!'

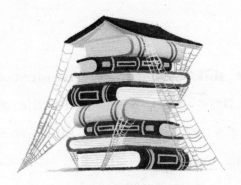

CHAPTER 5
ONE GOOD THING

The one good thing about the terrible news about the library was that, when the cleaning supplies were delivered, Reenie put them straight in the cupboard instead of grabbing the bug spray and spraying it here, there and everywhere. It was forgotten – thought unimportant –

in the shock, which gave Beancat a little more time. Also, because Reenie was all of a fluster, she didn't slide the door of the cupboard all the way across when closing it. There was no need to create a diversion.

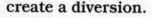

Furry Purry Beancat pretended that this was of no interest to her as she sauntered past, rubbing Reenie's legs. She had called the hiding of the bug spray *Operation Magic Bean*. This had nothing to do with being Beancat, but plenty to do with the hiding place she had in mind.

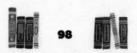

Everyone who came into the library seemed to have read the newspaper article too.

Mr Pasternak was outraged. 'I shall be *writink* a letter to the mayor, the local newspaper and the international press!' he declared.

Others offered their support.

When Yusuf arrived, he went straight up to Marcia at the counter.

'I am most unhappy to hear this news,' he said. 'You were all most welcoming yesterday and I was hoping to come here often. I am very saddened. Will you lose your employment, Marcia?'

'Don't you go worrying about me, Yusuf!' said Marcia. 'We're here – Gothport Library

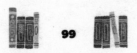

is here – to serve the community and *that's* what matters. We're not going without a fight.'

Beancat noticed Yusuf's expression change at the word 'fight'. 'Fight?' he asked. He sounded worried.

'Not with guns and barricades, Yusuf!' she added with a smile, 'but with people power and protest. We will have our voice heard.'

'I know that I am a newcomer and an outsider,' said Yusuf, 'but I would very much like to offer my services in helping you any way I can.'

'Thank you!' said Marcia. 'And you're not an outsider. You're in here, with us!'

Gregory had obviously been listening in

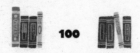

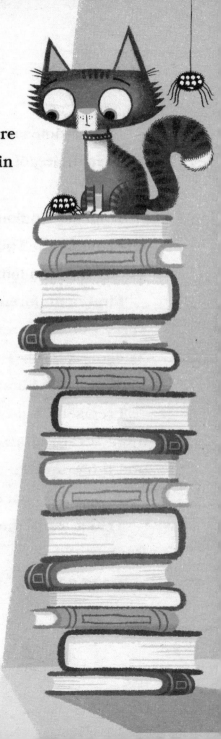

too. He and Beancat were on top of a bookstack in the non-fiction section.

'If the bug spray doesn't get us, the bulldozers will,' said Gregory with a spidery sigh. 'It seems that someone has it in for me.'

'Stop thinking about YOURSELF once in a while,' said Daphne, doing her regular – but still surprising – dropping-in-from-anywhere trick.

'Oh, pardon me for fearing for my own life,' said Gregory. 'How selfish of me to want to live.'

'What do we do, Furry?' asked Daphne, ignoring him. 'You were right about the library being in danger!'

'First and foremost, I knock the bug spray out of the cupboard,' said Beancat. 'Gregory's right. That's still a problem. As for saving the library, what *can* we do?'

'Precisely,' said Gregory, having let out a big breath of air. 'What CAN a fluffy cat and a few spiders do to help save a whole building? It's hopeless.'

'That's not the right attitude,' said Daphne. 'We—'

'We're doomed!' said Gregory.

'We n—'

'The library will be closed. Our home destroyed.'

'One thing I DO know,' said Beancat, 'is that moaning won't help.'

'Thank you for your words of wisdom,' said Gregory. 'If you hadn't said that I would have been CONVINCED that moaning would solve EVERYTHING and—'

Daphne blinked her many eyes and looked at Beancat. 'Sometimes I wonder why I ever married him,' she said.

Beancat nearly fell off the bookstack.

Daphne and Gregory were MARRIED?!?! To each other?!?!?

She did her best not to show her complete and utter surprise.

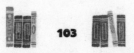

As well as class visits from three different schools in the morning, there was a meeting of the Reminiscence Group in the afternoon.

All the talk was about the plans to close the library. Teachers came to speak to Marcia and, when the children were stroking Furry Purry Beancat, they were saying things like:

'Who will love you like I do, Furry?'

'I will miss you SO much!'

'Where will you live, poor kitty?'

But VERY soon both grown-ups and children alike were saying, 'We can't let this happen!' and 'We WON'T let this happen!'

and 'This is OUR library!'

The Reminiscence Group was made up of older members of the community who met in the library regularly to talk about their memories of growing up in Gothport. But that particular Thursday all the talk was about the library itself.

There were cries of:

'We'll start a campaign!'
'We'll start a petition!'
'We'll hold protests!'

Little did they know, their conversations were being listened to with keen interest by a certain furry, purry cat and two spiders (one more gloomy than the other).

'Start a petition?' said Gregory. 'What's a petition?' He was spinning a new web across one of the ceiling lights near the enquiries desk. 'It's not some kind of fire, is it? They're not planning on starting a fire, are they? Fires usually end in disaster. We'll probably all be burnt to a crisp.'

'A petition?' said Daphne. 'I think it's a kind of wall. Perhaps they want to build a wall to keep the library-haters out. Humans seem very keen to build walls.'

'Knowing my luck, I'll be stuck on one side of the wall and you and our future spiderlings will be stuck on the other,' said Gregory.

'We're spiders,' said Daphne. 'We can get over any silly old wall.'

106

But Gregory wasn't listening. 'Or worse still, I'd be stuck with the spiderlings and you'd be on the other. How could I cope?'

'They can fend for themselves once they hatch,' Daphne pointed out. 'It's not as if you'd have to feed and burp them.'

'Yes, but—'

'You're thinking of a *partition*,' said Beancat, looking up from the windowsill. 'A *petition* is a list of signatures you get from people. The more the better.' She paused. *So Daphne and Gregory are expecting babies!* she thought. *That's nice.*

'What use is a list of signatures?' asked Gregory.

'Yes, what will they do with the list once they've got all the names?' Daphne said, a little embarrassed by the partition/petition confusion. In truth, she was extraordinarily knowledgeable for a spider. (That's what comes from spending your life in a library.)

'The petition shows how many people want to keep the library open, so the more signatures the better. Then they will probably hand it to the mayor,' said Beancat, 'to show her how unpopular her self-service library corner idea is!'

'Not the woman with the funny hat?' said Gregory. 'Do you remember her, Daphne? She came here to give out the prizes for

that writing competition.'

'When we were spiderlings? Of course! Had a hat like a sleeping rabbit on her head. Angelica Hayloft or some silly name like that.'

'Angela Haycroft,' said Beancat. 'Mayor Angela Haycroft. That was the name Reg read out of the paper.'

'That's it! You've met her, too, Furry,' said Daphne. 'At the prize-giving for the children's drawing competition, you were sitting on her chair and she got all annoyed about getting cat hairs on her skirt.'

Of course, Furry Purry Beancat *didn't* remember because she couldn't remember what had gone before when she woke up in one of her nine lives!

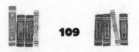

'Oh yes . . . how silly of me to forget!' she said, not wanting to seem odd. *Hmmm, this mayor doesn't sound very nice*, she thought. *What does a bit of Furry Purry Beancat hair on your clothes matter when you're giving out prizes to excited children?*

'Look!' said Gregory, all of his eyes wide open and up on all eight legs as alert as can be.

'What is it?' said Daphne.

'It's Reenie. She's heading for the front door!'

'Are you sure?' asked Beancat. She couldn't see out to the foyer from her position on the windowsill.

'Yes!' said Daphne. 'Okay, Furry! It's time

to put *Operation Magic Bean* into action!'

With Reenie out of the building for the first time since she'd arrived that morning, Furry Purry Beancat jumped down from the windowsill and dashed into the staffroom.

There was no one there.

It was now or never.

Furry Purry Beancat walked across the wooden floorboards, breathing in the smell of years and years, and layers and layers, of polish. She reached her target and was pleased to see the cupboard of cleaning products still had a gap between the edge of the sliding door and the frame where Reenie hadn't pulled it across fully.

Beancat slipped in her paw and pushed. This wasn't easy for a cat. The runners

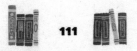

– the little 'track' on which the bottom of the door slid – seemed a little sticky and resistant to her efforts. She pushed again . . .

. . . then her super-cat hearing caused her ears to swivel and she picked up the sound of someone coming.

It was Dave.

'Hello, cat,' he said, eyeing Furry Purry Beancat suspiciously as he walked in. 'Are you up to no good?'

Why did it have to be Dave – the one human in the library who seemed not to like her – who had interrupted Furry's mission? Beancat started to wash, trying to look as innocent as possible. She paused, mid-lick, looked up at him and then carried on.

Dave fumbled in his coat pocket, which was hanging on a hook by the back door, took out whatever it was that he'd come in for and then left. He glanced back at Furry Purry as he went.

When Furry Purry Beancat was satisfied that he was far enough away, she got

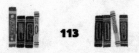

straight back to the matter in hand or, to be more accurate, straight back to the paw in the door!

She **PUUUUUUUUSHED** and the door stuttered open a bit more then, suddenly, glided freely along its runners. It was wide open.

And there, on the shelf, was a brand-new can of bug spray.

Beancat sat down with a plonk, lifted a front paw and swiped the can off the shelf. It hit the floor with a clatter and rolled a short way on its side. It was heavy but the perfect shape for her to butt with her head and steer with a paw to get it to roll in the direction she wanted.

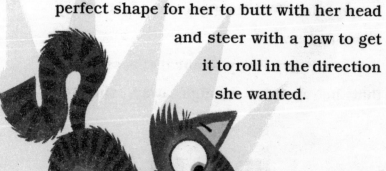

And that direction was the bottom of the weird and wonderful beanstalk. Apparently, it had once been part of a Jack and the Beanstalk display in the children's library, and when the display was changed the beanstalk took up permanent residence in the staffroom, being too good to throw away.

The beanstalk had been made to look as if it were sprouting from a small grassy mound made from Astroturf, like a plastic-grass blanket. During an earlier exploration of the room, Beancat had discovered a gap between the back of the mound and wall. Not only that, if she could get the bug-spray can in the gap, a loose flap of 'grass' could cover it! She could plant it like one of the

magic beans from which
the beanstalk grew in the
fairy tale!

This was the
hardest part but,
once she

had rolled the
can against the
wall, she was
able to push it
with her head

towards the beanstalk base . . .

Suddenly she heard the distinct footsteps of Marcia heading for the room!

Thinking quickly, Furry Purry Beancat lay down flat against the skirting, hiding the can behind her. She shut her eyes and concentrated hard on looking like she was fast asleep.

'You do choose some funny places for your cat-napping, Furry!' Marcia said with a chuckle as she walked into the staffroom. 'All this goin' on around you, and not a care in the world!'

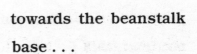

If you knew what was really going on, you wouldn't believe it, thought Beancat, keeping her eyes firmly closed.

Lying on a large can of bug spray to keep it hidden wasn't the most comfortable position to be in, but it didn't take long for Beancat's pretend nap to turn into real sleeping. Cats are such professional sleepers. When she awoke, she found herself alone again.

Furry Purry Beancat got to her feet, *stretched*, then got straight back to pushing the bug spray behind the beanstalk base . . .

Success! She managed to get it in the gap and the loose flap of pretend grass hid it perfectly.

Her furry, purry body swelled with pride. She'd had a plan. She'd put it into action and it had worked. *Operation Magic Bean* was a total success. Daphne and Gregory were safe for now.

If only saving the library could be so easy!

CHAPTER 6
THE MEETING

The first meeting of the Save Gothport Library campaign wasn't held in the library itself because, as Marcia explained, this was against council rules. It was held in the local Scout hut, instead. It had been built after the Second World War as a temporary building with a corrugated-iron roof, but was still standing nearly eighty years later. And it was packed. All the chairs were being sat on and people were standing round the edges and in the aisles.

There was a very small 'stage' at one end, with three chairs and a lectern. Marcia the librarian sat in one, a man with short stubbly hair, who was wearing a save libraries T-shirt, sat next to her, and next to him was a woman wearing an extraordinary hat and a huge mayoral chain of office (in other words, a chunky gold mayor's chain).

So YOU'RE Mayor Angela Haycroft, thought Furry Purry Beancat, who was sitting in the front row. Well, to be more accurate, she was sitting on Reg the caretaker's lap who was sitting in the front row.

The meeting started with Marcia welcoming everyone and thanking them for coming. Then she introduced the mayor, who made her way to the lectern.

There was a smattering of applause: a few polite claps rather than a real welcome.

'Thank you,' she said, though her expression suggested that there was a nasty smell VERY close to her nose. 'I am here this evening to say that there is absolutely NO need to have a Save Gothport Library campaign when you will not be losing your library. A new centre will be built housing a swimming pool, health spa and self-service library corner, launching Gothport Leisure into the twenty-first century . . .'

Those are exactly the same words Reg

read out of the newspaper, thought Furry Purry Beancat.

'What's a self-service library corner?' shouted someone in the audience.

'An entire corner of the building dedicated to library services, which members of the community will be able to access and use without the reliance on staff—' began the mayor.

'An entire corner is still just a corner!' someone interrupted.

'And what "library services"?' shouted someone at the back.

'Er, borrowing books, I suppose,' said the mayor.

'Zere is much more to libraries zan books, Mayor Haycroft!' said a man.

125

Furry Purry Beancat recognized *that* voice. She raised her head. *You tell 'em, Mr Pasternak!* she thought.

There was a cheer from the audience.

'And what do you mean, please, when you say without the reliance on staff?' asked Yusuf, standing up in the front row. He'd been sitting right next to Reg and Furry Purry Beancat. 'You say this as though it's a good thing. But librarians are what make libraries libraries!'

There was a big CHEER from the audience.

Mayor Angela Haycroft looked far from happy. 'I don't know if you're from around here,' she said, glaring at Yusuf, 'but—'

Marcia was having none of this and

leapt to her feet. 'Mr Abadi is a user of the library, which is more than can be said of many of those making decisions about its future . . .' She glared at the mayor.

There was another cheer.

Mrs Haycroft raised her hands for silence. 'You will have a new swimming pool!' she said firmly. 'There will be running machines! And a self-service library corner! It'll be part of a whole new leisure complex in Grant Road.'

'Grant Road? But that's two bus rides away!' wailed Joan.

Just then, Furry Purry Beancat's super-cat eyesight caught the tiniest glint above the mayor's hat . . . It was light reflecting the thinnest strand of silken thread.

Of *spider* thread.

And at the end of that thread was Gregory, slowly lowering himself.

How on earth has he got here? Furry Purry Beancat thought. Then she remembered the tickle in her tail she'd felt on the way over, as she'd lain draped across Reg's shoulders. *Had Gregory been hitching a ride in her fur?* She grinned to herself. *The cheek of it!*

She watched in awe as Gregory came nearer and nearer his target, then disappeared behind Angela Haycroft's head.

That was when the mayor screamed and started flailing her arms about and reaching back to her collar.

Gregory must have managed to slip down inside her clothes and run around her back because his victim was now doing the most extraordinary dance across the stage.

Beancat's biggest concern was for Gregory's safety. He might easily get squashed!

Marcia had run over to the mayor to try to find out what was wrong.

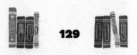

'Are you all right, Mayor Haycroft?' she asked with concern.

'You did this!' spat the mayor, jiggling about. 'I don't know what or how, but you did this! And you would do well to be careful what you say,' she said, her voice much lower so the audience wouldn't hear her, though swivel-eared Beancat did. Loud and clear. 'As someone working for the council you should think very carefully about speaking publicly against it . . . or who knows what might happen!'

At that exact moment Beancat saw that Gregory had somehow got free of the mayor's clothes and was scuttling across the floor of the stage. The trouble was,

Mayor Haycroft spotted him at the exact same time.

She raised her foot to stamp on him.

Furry Purry Beancat was off Reg's lap before you could say 'Bitey Scratchy Beancat', which was what Beancat had become. She hurled herself on to the stage or, more accurately, directly on to the mayor.

Instead of stamping on Gregory, Angela Haycroft toppled backwards, grappling with a terrifying furball of teeth and claw. She landed unceremoniously on her bottom with a bump.

Her job done, Furry Purry Beancat became Furry Purry Beancat again, jumping elegantly off the mayor and strutting off with head and tail held high.

Reg looked on in horror, wondering what had made his beloved cat behave that way (not that he liked the mayor one bit), and Marcia was helping the mayor to her feet. The mood of the room, however, was very much on the side of a certain FPB.

'*Beancat! Beancat! Beancat!*' shouted the audience, jumping to their feet and

clapping. It soon became a chant! 'Beancat! Beancat! Beancat!'

A man in a brown suit who'd been sitting in the front row on the other side of the aisle to Beancat, Yusuf and Reg now got to his feet, picked up Angela Haycroft's hat, and stepped up on to the stage, steering her to the fire exit.

'Forget their silly little campaign,' Mayor Haycroft hissed to him, almost spitting her words out. 'And when their ancient library closes its doors for the last time, I want that cat put in a cat home.'

Beancat heard every word.

There were cheers at the mayor's departure.

The man with the stubbly hair and the

Save Libraries T-shirt stood up and walked to the lectern. 'Hi, everyone,' he said. 'After all this excitement, it's time to talk tactics. My name's Brian Ibbotson and I'm from the national Save Libraries campaign . . .'

Furry Purry Beancat took the opportunity to follow Angela Haycroft and the man through the fire exit. She found herself on a short path running diagonally across a small patch of grass.

'Pssst!'

Furry Purry Beancat looked around but saw no one.

'Pssst!' said the voice again.

Beancat looked around a second time.

'I'm here, you annoying purrball!'

Now who would speak to her like that?

Aha! Only Graham the children's library mouse, of course. 'Where are you, Graham?' she meowed.

Graham appeared from behind a tuft of grass at the edge of the path. 'Here! Honestly, I thought cats were supposed to have good eyesight!'

'What are you doing here?'

'You're not the only one who's worried about the library. It's my family's home too, you know.'

'Of course,' said Beancat. 'Sorry.'

'And it's lucky I came,' he said. 'Look who I've rescued!'

Furry Purry Beancat moved closer and there, on the mouse's back, was Gregory!

'Gregory!' Furry said. 'You're alive!'

137

'Only just!' said the spider, sounding very sorry for himself.

'He's fine,' said Graham, 'apart from a kink in one leg.'

'Such a relief,' said Gregory, not sounding in the slightest bit relieved. 'I had no idea you were a doctor.'

'That was a very, *very* silly thing you did back there,' said Beancat. 'Why on earth did you do it?'

'Because I didn't like that Angela Haycroft and the things she was saying about our lovely library. I couldn't stand idly by and twiddle my thumbs.'

'Spiders don't have thumbs,' Graham pointed out.

Gregory chose to ignore him. 'And the four good things spiders are good at are: spinning and weaving, catching dinner, tickling people and frightening them!'

Gregory climbed off Graham, limping slightly, and made his way a short distance across the path before climbing up Furry Purry Beancat's leg. 'Thank you, Graham. Not that I was necessarily worth rescuing . . .'

'My pleasure.' The mouse replied. 'And you did a very brave thing, Gregory.'

'Yes, you did,' agreed Beancat. 'A very brave but DANGEROUS thing. Heaven

knows what Daphne will have to say about it.'

'True,' said Gregory. 'And, Beancat?'

'Yes, Gregory?'

'Thank you for saving my life.'

CHAPTER 7
NEW BEGINNINGS

Daphne didn't have anything to say about it because, when Furry Purry Beancat and Gregory got back to the library – with Graham dashing off ahead – they found that she had just laid her eggs. And there were hundreds of them!

Daphne had made a silk spider-thread

mattress for them to lie on and was now busy weaving them a silk blanket to go on top.

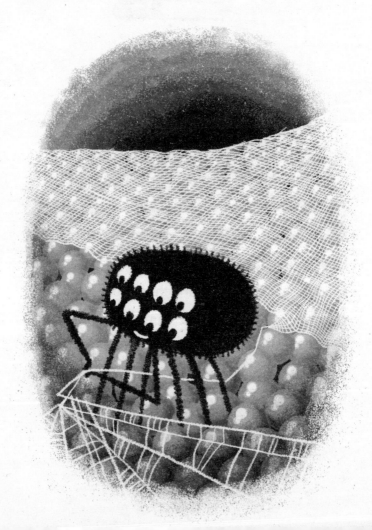

Furry Purry Beancat had never seen anything like it. Then again, she may well have done, of course, but she had no memory of it!

'Can I help?' asked Gregory.

Daphne paused for a moment and turned to look at him unblinkingly with all her eyes. 'Do I ever ask for your help when weaving is involved?'

'No, my dove!' said Gregory meekly.

She turned back to her weaving.

It's such delicate work, thought Furry Purry Beancat. *So fast and skilful.*

In next to no time Daphne and Gregory's eggs were covered by the silk mattress beneath and the silk blanket above, but Daphne's work didn't end there. She

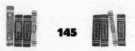

145

carried on weaving.

'What's she doing now?' Beancat asked Gregory from a safe distance, not wishing to disturb the new mum.

'She's making an egg sac to hang them up in,' said Gregory. 'Lucky that's not my job. I'd probably mess it up and it would fall and squash them all before they'd even hatched.'

They were in Reg the caretaker's room. The one which had, over the years, become storage for broken bits of library furniture and discarded bits and bobs that the staff didn't know what to do with but didn't want to throw away.

To do her best to protect her eggs and future hatchlings from Reenie and any

bug spray she might get, Daphne had gone far back in the pile, near a wall. Furry Purry Beancat would probably never have found her without Gregory. She'd had to **SQUEEEEEEZE** through the gaps between the furniture – chairs, tables, an enormous roll-top desk – like a slippery eel.

It's easy to forget that Furry Purry Beancat is, in truth, a lot slimmer than she looks, so can slip through much tighter spaces than you might imagine. It's because so much of her is furry, purry FUR!

Suddenly, Beancat felt a sneeze rising in her nose. Well, there was LOTS of dust around! She worried it might be the sort of sneeze that would scatter an egg sac, silk mattress, silk blanket and hundreds

of spider eggs to the four winds. So she turned round as quickly as possible to sneeze in the opposite direction, and lost her footing on the leg of broken chair, tumbling forward in a most un-ladylike, un-catlike, un-Beancatlike manner!

'There you go again,' sighed Gregory.

'Thank you,' said Daphne, who realized that Beancat must have taken a dive rather than sneeze over her precious darling eggs.

Beancat had come to rest on what looked like the top crust of a large oval pie with crimped edges.

This was no pie crust. It was cold, like stone. Beancat could make out some of the words carved into it. There was a name – LADY FRANCIS MULHOLLAND – and the phrase GRANTED IN PERPETUITY TO, followed by more writing half hidden by furniture.

'Any idea who Lady Francis Mulholland is or was?' she asked Gregory, having read what she could see of the pie-crust-shaped thingummy.

'Mulholland?' asked Gregory in obvious surprise. 'Why, Daphne's family is called Mulholland.'

WHAT? thought Beancat in surprise. *How strange is THAT?*

Daphne did her trick of dropping down on a silk thread, as if appearing out of nowhere. 'Yup. It's true. Any spider born in the library foyer has traditionally been a Mulholland.'

'Have you finished the egg sac?' asked Gregory.

'Yes, all done,' said Daphne. 'I'm exhausted.'

Her husband scuttled off to look at her handiwork.

'Why's he limping?' asked Daphne.

'A long story,' said Furry Purry Beancat. 'Congratulations on laying all those eggs.'

'Thank you,' said Daphne. 'Why were you asking about the name Mulholland?'

'It's written here,' said Beancat. 'And why are spiders born in the foyer called Mulholland?'

'I suppose because that plaque you're standing on must be the one that used to be on the wall of the foyer a long, long time ago, back in the days of my however-many-times-great-grandparents.'

'Must it?'

'Yes, apparently there used to be a Mulholland plaque out there,' said Daphne, 'with lots of webs woven in and around

it. It's part of the spider folklore of this library.'

'Have you any idea what *perpetuity* means?' asked Beancat, who is not only a surprisingly knowledgeable cat but also one who can read, which is rarer still. But she can't be expected to know the meaning of *every* word. Who does, human or feline?

'I'm afraid not. Now, forgive me, Furry, but I'm exhausted and need to get some sleep.'

'You do that,' said Furry Purry Beancat. 'Sleep well.'

That night, Beancat herself didn't sleep well. She kept on worrying that she would

wake up the next day and find herself in another of her nine lives without having saved the library!

Fortunately for all, that didn't happen and the following morning Beancat patrolled the foyer before any of the staff arrived. There was no sign of where the plaque in Reg's room might once have been fixed to the wall. Although there were posters and a corkboard and a fire-alarm panel, all of which could be hiding evidence of where it once had been.

She inspected the black-and-white tiles on the floor. They were old but still remarkably clean considering the number of boots and shoes that must have traipsed over them in all weathers over many, many years.

Something was niggling in the back of Furry Purry Beancat's mind, which made her do a patrol of the whole library. In the local history section she looked up at the old map of the county and then across to the brown-and-white photo. In the old days, before colour photos, they were in black and white and before that, in the very early days of photography, brown and white.

And this was the one with a BROWN-AND-WHITE FLOOR!

THAT'S what I've had in the back of my mind, thought Furry Purry Beancat and she started purring very loudly.

Beancat jumped up on to a nearby table to take a closer look. Then she ambled up

a pile of large bound copies of old local newspapers.

She stood on her back legs and stretched right up, her two front paws against the wall; her nose just reached the bottom quarter of the old, old photo.

Not only was the photo itself very old, the glass and the frame were both yellowed with age.

She studied what she could of the picture very closely indeed. There was no doubt about it. The photograph had been taken in the foyer. It looked very different, and there was the plaque about Lady Francis Mulholland on the wall, but it was, without question, the foyer of Gothport Library.

In the picture a woman was standing to the side of the plaque, her head turned towards it. She was wearing a long dress and a funny hat with thin pointy feathers sticking out of it. To the other side of the plaque stood a man with a top hat and an enormous beard. Because the photo was so old and the beard so big, the man looked more beard than anything else.

There was some writing on a white strip below the photo, but the ink had faded over the years, the glass was yellowing and, truth be told, Furry Purry Beancat found it hard enough reading printed letters. Handwriting was far harder.

Reg would be here soon and the others soon after, so Beancat jumped down and ambled over to the staffroom to greet him on arrival.

The talk in the staffroom that morning, when Marcia, ginger-haired Lizzie and Dave had arrived, was all about the meeting in the Scout hut.

'That Mayor Haycroft was so horrible,' said Dave.

'You won't 'ear no argument from me,'

said Marcia, who was usually nice about everyone.

Furry Purry Beancat sat on Reg's lap. She knew now that the dark blue suit he wore every day was part of his caretaker's uniform. She thought he looked VERY SMART and he always brushed his trousers with a clothes brush he hung on the back of his office door after Furry Purry Beancat had left him covered in fur! She loved sitting on his lap and he loved having her there. As he stroked her, he would sometimes talk about Jean who, she soon realized, must have been Reg's wife who had died some years before. She sensed his love and sadness. Furry Purry Beancat was glad that she was there to give him LOTS of love. But that morning all the talk was of how to try to save the library.

Later, the schoolchildren arrived and Beancat leapt into action. She needed to find out more about that plaque. She let herself be petted and greeted by all the children, but it was Timmy she was waiting to see.

Hello, Furry Purry Beancat, he said in her mind.

Good morning, Timmy! said Beancat. *I need your help. It's important.*

Of course, said Timmy excitedly. *What can I do?* He was stroking her as they spoke.

I need you to ask your teacher what 'in perpetuity' means.

Perp-e-tu-ity?

That's it, said Beancat.

Of course, said Timmy. He gave Beancat a scratch between the ears, stood up and turned to Jenny, his one-to-one helper who spoke sign language with her hands.

He spelled out 'perpetuity' with his hands letter by letter, and then asked her what it meant.

Jenny replied quickly, her fingers moving at speed.

Timmy crouched back down and stroked Furry Purry Beancat under the chin. She did her VERY best to take in what Timmy was saying, but was more than a little distracted by the under-the-chin scratching, which was BLISSSSSSSSSSSS! She almost went into an overdrive of purring.

Jenny says that 'in perpetuity' means forever, he told her.

Forever? Beancat echoed, her purr calming down as she started to consider what that meant. *Now THAT, Timmy, is very interesting. Thank you.*

If the inscription on the plaque shown in the photograph, and now Reg's room, meant what Furry Purry Beancat *thought*

it meant, this could change EVERYTHING. She would have to bring it to everyone's attention!

Now, Furry Purry Beancat was very good at making plans – you will know that from *Operation Magic Bean* – but sometimes the quickest way to get a result, especially when time is running out, is to ACT QUICKLY. And this is how *Operation Crash Bang Wallop* came into being.

She had gathered all the information she required and now she had to share it. She looked around the library.

Mr Pasternak sat in his usual place at the corner desk, writing to everyone he could think of who might be able to help in the fight to save the library.

Yusuf was sitting in the newspaper section but ignoring the newspapers. He was writing some very large letters on a very large square of cardboard.

The Reminiscence Group were sitting round their usual table but, instead of talking about sherbet dips and ration books, they were having a council of war against the new leisure centre with its unstaffed 'library corner'.

Joan was poring over bus timetables and working out distances with Marcia at the library counter, while Reenie had her yellow feather duster out and was doing the tops of the doors.

It was time to act. Suddenly, and without warning, Beancat put *Operation Crash*

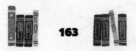

Bang Wallop into action. She dashed like a fireball of furry-purriness across the library, into the local history section, on to the table, on to the local newspapers and LAUNCHED herself up at the old photo.

She hit it at speed and clung on to the frame for dear life . . . dislodging it from the wall.

It fell with an almighty CRASH, the frame breaking into two Ls and the glass shattering into jagged pieces. Fortunately, Beancat jumped clear in time, avoiding injury.

People dashed from all corners of the library to see what had happened.

Beancat just sat there, half a metre from the damage, licking her front paws as though she didn't have a care in the world. Little did anyone realize that what looked like chaos and mayhem was the result of a carefully laid plan!

'What've you done, Furry?' asked Marcia in surprise.

CHAPTER 8
HELP ACROSS THE YEARS

While Reg (wearing a pair of tough work gloves) was carefully picking up the larger pieces of yellowed glass off the floor and putting them into a metal bin, Marcia was retrieving the photograph. She held one corner and lifted it carefully, shaking it so that any smaller pieces of glass might fall off.

'What got into you, girl?' she asked Beancat.

'You haven't behaved like that since you were a kitten,' said Reg, 'when you used to go crazy and shoot up the curtains!'

Furry Purry Beancat sat a short distance away, but she wasn't purring. *It's very nice of you not to be annoyed with me,* she thought. *But I do wish you'd LOOK AT THE PHOTOGRAPH.*

When planning *Operation Crash Bang Wallop,* Furry Purry Beancat had thought of trying to get Timmy to show them the photo. Or having Gregory and Daphne hang down in front of it so that Reenie might try brushing them away and see what was in the picture. But, in the end, she had decided on the direct approach: her SMASHING idea!

'Is the picture damaged?' asked Reg.

'No, it seems fine,' said Marcia, looking at it properly for the first time. 'In fact, this old photo is in much better condition than I imagined. It must have been the glass that made it look so faded.'

'You can even read the writing on that plaque between those two people,' said

Reg, peering over her shoulder. He pointed and read it out loud.

LADY FRANCIS
MULHOLLAND
bequeathed this building
& the land upon which it stands
IN PERPETUITY TO
THE PEOPLE OF GOTHPORT
for use as a free public library
on this day, 4 July
MDCCCLXVIII

Marcia looked at Reg.

Reg looked at Marcia.

Furry Purry Beancat watched them both and began to purr.

 170

Marcia hurried over to the desk where Mr Pasternak was working. She lay the huge photo over the papers in front of him. 'I'm sorry to interrupt, Mr Pasternak,' she said. 'No. That's not true. I'm not sorry. Would you read this please?' She pointed.

He read, a smile slowly spreading across his face.

'"In perpetuity" means forever, am I right?' said Marcia. 'So this is saying that Lady Mulholland – whoever she was and God bless her soul – gave this library to the town FOREVER?'

'I think it is much better than that,' said Mr Pasternak in his thick accent. 'There will have been deeds and a contract and in

law "in perpetuity" means even *beyond* the contract.'

'So even if the councils somehow managed to *change* the contract or the deeds, they can't alter the fact that this building *has* to remain a free public library?'

'Precisely.'

Marcia grabbed both sides of Mr Pasternak's head and kissed the top of it. 'I'm s-s-so sorry!' she said, as she realized what she'd just done. 'I don't know what came over me!'

'That's quite all right!' said the elderly gentleman. 'We have much to celebrate!'

Hearing loud, happy voices, Yusuf came over to see what all the excitement was about. They told him.

'You have local newspapers going back many years, do you not?' he asked quietly.

'Almost two hundred years,' said Lizzie, who'd now joined the group. 'Why?'

'Well, surely such a splendid event as this good lady giving the townsfolk a new library would be recorded in the newspaper?'

'Of course!' said Marcia, a chuckle rising in her throat. 'But what year is MDCCCLXVIII?'

'That is easy,' said Yusuf. 'It is 1868.'

'What a team!' said Marcia happily. 'We'll save this library yet.'

Beancat slipped away to the staff area and to Reg's room to report the latest to Gregory and Daphne.

'It worked!' she told them. 'I think the library WILL be saved.'

'There's still plenty of time for something to go terribly wrong,' said Gregory and, although the words were just the sort of gloomy thing he would say, he sounded a little half-hearted, as if he couldn't hide just how *pleased* he really was.

'Quiet, you!' said Daphne, dropping in from above.

'How are your eggs?' asked Beancat.

'Fine thanks, Furry. There's nothing to do now. They'll hatch when they're good and ready.'

'Which still leaves the problem of Reenie and the first Thursday of NEXT month,'

said Gregory. The library may be saved, but we could still be goners. Dead. Departed. No more.'

Daphne skedaddled over to her husband. 'Beancat told me you did a very brave thing last night, frightening off that dreadful Mayor Haycroft, and I know you will do all you can to protect our children.'

If spiders could blush, that's what Gregory would be doing right now, thought Beancat.

The rest of the morning was a flurry of activity. Sure enough, amongst the bound copies of the *Gothport Chronicle* in the local history section, Yusuf found the 9 July 1868 edition, which contained a very interesting article about Lady Mulholland bequeathing the library to the town at its grand opening.

There was much backslapping and whoops of excitement and triumph and joy!

The disliker of cats, Dave, stared at Furry Purry Beancat, who was sitting on an oak chair nearby.

'Do you know,' he said to no one in particular, 'I wouldn't be at all surprised if Furry had deliberately knocked that painting off the wall to make us look at it . . .'

Marcia laughed. 'That would be something, wouldn't it?' she said. 'LIBRARY SAVED BY INCREDIBLE READING CAT!'

'Mistress Beancat is certainly a most excellent cat,' said Yusuf, looking up from the newspaper spread out before him. 'Which reminds me. I received this today.'

From his pocket he produced a blue envelope and from the envelope he pulled out a photograph of a beautiful cat standing in the rubble of a building. 'This is my Iishraq. She is alive and well, as is my cousin Abida who cares for her.'

Furry Purry Beancat jumped up on to his lap and rested her chin on the edge of the table, her nose almost touching the glossy picture.

She's your Sunshine, she purred.

The happy moment was interrupted by Reenie running towards them. 'You're not going to believe it. You are NOT going to believe it.'

'What? What is it? You okay, Reenie?' asked Marcia.

'I am fine. Tickety-boo! Plump currant! On this very day that Furry has led us to the photograph of that library-saving plaque, a spider has just led me to the plaque itself!'

'Are you sure you haven't been affected by cleaning-fluid fumes?' joked Lizzie.

'It's true!' said Reenie, her Scottish accent coming through loud and strong. 'It turns out that the plaque has been here all this time under all that junk in Reg's room! I was chasing a couple of spiders across the floor with my feather duster and they led me right to it. I wouldn't even have recognized it if I hadn't just seen it in that photo.'

'What a day of happy chances!' said Mr Pasternak.

'Chances?' said Reenie indignantly, rubbing the enamel Scottish thistle pinned to her housecoat. 'I'll have you know that a spider plays a very important part in my people's history, giving Robert the Bruce the inspiration to carry on his fight and by protecting him from his enemies!'

'You've changed your tune!' Reg laughed. 'You've been having a constant battle with spiders and their webs over the years and suddenly they're heroic Scottish beasties!' He tickled Furry Purry Beancat's furry, purry chin.

'Yes, well, maybe I should have remembered my Scottish heritage!' said

Reenie. 'I think those spiders wanted to save this library as much as we did! I'll keep this place clear of cobwebs but, from now on, all spiders are welcome!'

'You daft thing!' said Reg kindly. He looked down at Furry Purry Beancat on his lap. 'If anyone saved this library it was my Beancat . . . Now, come on, let's go and get that plaque.'

That evening, when the library was closed and the last of the sun cast patterns of light on to the carpet between the bookstacks, Furry Purry Beancat and her two eight-legged friends looked back at their event-filled day.

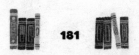

'You do realize that you saved the library, Furry,' said Daphne.

'Not just me,' she said. 'It was a team effort. And you two saved your children – *all* the spiders in the library – from bug spray.'

'We did, didn't we?' said Gregory. 'Of course, I knew about Robert the Spruce all along and that Reenie is Scottish and—'

'Nice try, husband!' said Daphne, 'but no, you didn't. And, anyway, it's Robert the *Bruce* not *Spruce*.'

'Ah,' said Gregory, 'but if I had known about it . . .'

'You're welcome in the children's library any time,' said a small voice that Beancat recognized at once. 'All of you.'

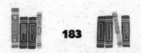

'Thank you, Graham,' she said.

Furry Purry Beancat purred and padded off, leaving them to it. She had a feeling her work here was done.

She found a patch of sunlight, followed her tail round in a circle three times, then settled herself down in a furry ball of purry cat. She yawned, lowered her head to the

ground and pulled her beautiful, fluffy tail
in front of her little pink nose.

Where will I wake up next? she wondered,
slowly closing her big green eyes and
drifting off to sleep . . .

PHILIP ARDAGH

Roald Dahl-Funny-Prize-winning author **PHILIP ARDAGH** has been published for around thirty years, written more than 100 titles and been translated into forty languages. Books range from his bestselling and international award-winning Eddie Dickens adventures — celebrating twenty years in 2020 — to his prize-winning Grubtown Tales, the Grunt series, illustrated by Axel Scheffler, and *High in the Clouds*, a collaboration with Sir Paul McCartney, currently being developed as a film by Netflix.

ROB BIDDULPH is a bestselling and multi award-winning author/illustrator and was the official World Book Day Illustrator for 2020. His first picture book, *Blown Away*, won the Waterstones Children's Book Prize in 2015. His second book, *GRRRRR!* was nominated for the CILIP Greenaway Medal and the IBW Children's Picture Book of the Year in 2016.

DON'T MISS ALL THE ADVENTURES OF . . .

THE NINE LIVES OF
FURRY PURRY
BEANCAT

THE REAL

FURRY PURRY BEANCAT

PHILIP ARDAGH didn't have a pet as a child, except when looking after the class tadpole one weekend. He was in his twenties when he got his very first pet, a long-haired tabby-and-white cat called Beany. 'I loved her to bits!' he said. 'She was very furry and very purry!' Beany lived into her eighteenth year and, in creaky old age, sat with Philip in his study as he wrote. One day, it occurred to him that – if he slightly skewed the meaning of a cat having nine lives – she could have

eight other exciting lives ... and the idea of **THE NINE LIVES OF FURRY PURRY BEANCAT** was born.